The Bouquet

Ricky Boone

ANDREA JOHNSON BOOKS PUBLISHING

PURCHASE THESE OTHER BOOKS BY RICKY BOONE

PILLOW TALK

JUICE BOX

Stay tuned for more books by Ricky Boone

Coming soon!

GUNS AND BUTTER

THE DERANGED

THINK LIKE A HOE

Visit the publishing website to find out more about Ricky Boone and his upcoming books!

www.Ajbpublishing.com

The Bouquet

Cover art designed by Andrea Johnson Books Publishing.

First published by Andrea Johnson Books Publishing. 04/28/2021

6565 N. MacArthur Blvd, Suite 225 Dallas, TX. 75039
www.Ajbpublishing.com

ISBN: 978-0-578-89949-7

Black Magic

I could just rest in you
While you breathe in my ear
Stop all erotic motion just so you could feel my pulse from
there
I can feel you dripping down my thigh
Like a running tear from an open eye
It's been a long time coming
So I don't ask questions like why do pigs fly high
Digging into you softly
Is like my loins soaking into an edible
You're incredible
I'm feeling your complex
And it's not all about the sex
As your fountains rush over my heavy mountains and
crush the waves. Pushing me into your dark caves of
Judah
You never caught the Bouquet
You've never even carried it before...
Your better then scales
Hidden behind these close doors
Or the liquor poured into the pores of these blunt
smoking whores. I filled up daily with my seeds
That bleed envy to succeed but just breathe on the
couches and receive all men needs
You're more than that to me
You're more than a vision You're reality
And it's magic baby. Black and soft and mushy
Thick sweet like yams
And taste so rich And they feel it
You get that greater me
Black magic..

4

Forgive me

It's too bad things didn't work out... now all we have of the past and the taste of my touch in your mouth. I was stuck in my feelings, and I didn't care...you coming back and then leave back and I knew it wasn't working hell... love with us was never going nowhere, loving you was doing nothing but re-breaking my heart and it wasn't fair. I thought that I could find it over there...but loving her cost a deep tare, she was more like a risk or a dare. But she spoke things you could only imagine; our lust became love even though she was a best friend of yours, you had a heart that could never budge. And filled with grudge, you didn't know how to love... but you knew how to one night. You couldn't get enough. But you struggled to sacrifice. My first wife couldn't get right. you thought you had it, but it was never in you to stay still or keep tight. I yearn for karma to hit you in the high light...but I won't wait...I'll know by the stress and expressions on your face...right...no more flashback of back shots or hash tags of dirty flicks that you use to dig, sipping on cotton candy, till we spread a towel on the couch and drained ourselves from the stains of ourselves. I loved you, but you just loved my sex. I wanted you, but you had a complex. Then your friend got into this boat and got a taste test, she craved me daily with a face fest. I was her fetish, now you regret it. I be that blessing you cry that replenish.

But then it was the Cake lady, that butter milk cream. Who would scream whenever I slept in between. So sweet I was sleep, too bad I couldn't keep her. My one night became a one month and two week with her. The first love I won't even speak on. All ppl would have to do is see her. Just imagine if my wood could only speak, my heart would argue with my piece, only if id listen to my spirit, I'd reap peace. I got lost during my search for love, laying down with these...lost souls in these streets...She was one I should have never touched again or went back for again or even loved again ...Lord forgive me.

Acknowledgements

First off I would like to acknowledge God, then my mother Dorothy Osborne, for being there for me and Grandparents as well as my uncle Darrell and late aunt Germaine my brother Johnathan and james Bishop Fredric Buford and my sister Jaylnne. Kevin wicker and his wife Kenesha, Brandon Macky, Marcus Grey shani and crystal Brown Palasek Laurence Pellot for being there through all my trials and I cannot forget Diana Buford as well. Blessings to you all for not judging me and believing in all I do. And last but not least, to all my Facebook followers for making this possible. So now if you really want to know the good and bad about a brother walk in life, read this book...

\- *Ricky Boone*

Table of Contents

The Bouquet

Ricky Boone

Part One

The Seed of a Baby Momma

Chapter One

Jermaine Taylor's thoughts brought back the memories in full detail, as he dwelled on the past....

'It was funny how we hooked up. Sixteen years old and calling ourselves in love, and only knowing one another for a few months.

She was a lot different from the girls I'd ever talked to. She had a three year old son at the age of sixteen. But she was unique to me. Her name was Tamar, Tamar Green. Seeing this girl was like seeing a full grown woman. She was like twenty five years old at the age of sixteen. Thighs, hips and booty, the whole package.

I instantly fell in love at Wick's Park on a fourth of July.

While hanging with my homeboys smoking a joint behind a bathroom building, that's when she pulled up.....'

***

"We smell it, what yaw smokin on?" Tamar said as she approached. Jermaine's boy Eric replied to her.

"That skunk. What's good with yaw? Yaw trying to smoke?"

Tamar's homegirl Shawntell replied to him.

"Hell yeah! If it's straight green."

Jermaine responded, while staring directly at Tamar. "Yeah, it's straight green." He spoke as he continued to roll up a joint.

Eric passed the joint he was already smoking to Shawntell. Suddenly Tamar broke the silence.

"This night is nice, ain't nobody trying to fight, everyone's chillin. Man, it's all good."

"Right." Jermaine replied to her.

They continued to smoke, passing the joint around to one another.

"What yaw got up for tonight?" Said Eric.

You see Eric already knew Shawntell and Tamar from school and around the way. Jermaine was from Grand Rapids visiting for the summer.

It's funny how weed can draw people together, because for the rest of that summer, Jermaine and Tamar became very close. To the point they found themselves sneaking out alone. And at times he would climb in through Tamar's bedroom window at night, just to get a taste.

Until one day, Jermaine was caught in the middle of their creep by Tamar's foster mother.

"What the hell is goin on!" Mrs. Green shouted, and clicked on the light.

"Oh my god!" Tamar said in shock.

"Jesus!" Jermaine shouted, knowing he was caught.

Tamar's mother started immediately throwing things, while Jermaine scrambled to pull up his boxers.

"Where in the hell you think you're going?" Her mother shouted at him, as Jermaine attempted to climb out the window.

"I'm a call the police. Sit your behind here while I go get the phone, then you can call your people.

Jermaine sat in the room, stricken, as he watched Tamar's mother beat her with a belt all in her back. More so because they'd had sex in the room, while the baby was sleeping on the floor on a pallet.

Mrs. Green gave Jermaine the phone to call his aunt Bonita, and explain to her what had just taken place.

Mrs. McCreed later on arrived to pick up Jermaine from Tamar's house.

"What in god's name are you doing at this woman's house?!" Jermaine's aunt shouted at him. He replied while looking down at his feet.

"She asked me to come over, and one thing led to another, and then we got caught."

"You must think I'm stupid or something." Mrs. McCreed responded. "You damn kids wasn't planning on watching TV at one in the morning. Jermaine, you ain't nothing but seventeen. And her ass, what? Sixteen with a damn three year old. She's asking for another baby if you're not careful."

Jermaine dropped his head again and nodded as if he understood what his aunt was saying.

But he really didn't care. He loved Tamar. Even though he knew he was about to be sent back to Michigan, all due to what just went down.

Chapter two

A few years had blown by, and Tamar was a thing of the past. Jermaine had found another love by the name of Juanita Boyde. Juanita was a very well educated church girl, who went back and got her G.E.D after dropping out of high school, due to having a child at an early age.

However, Juanita was a church girl with a little bit of crazy in her. But like most people, everyone has a dark side to them that others tend to overlook.

Jermaine was now married to Juanita, at the young age of twenty one. They were a young couple in love but with many problems. Her family was always in their business, or her insecurities. Or issues with Jermaine keeping a steady job because he'd just purchased them a home. However, things began to crash when the employment problems became a crisis.

The situation couldn't get any better because they'd already had two kids. And added to that, Juanita had another one on the way.

"I need some damn help! This is frustrating." Jermaine complained one day. He was tired and feeling overwhelmed.

"What you mean you need some help?" Juanita replied to him, looking at him like he was crazy.

"I mean help with this house, our home. I understand that you can't or don't want to work at all, but damn, at least try to keep the house clean or straighten up!" Jermaine argued in frustration.

Juanita immediately took offense to his remarks.

"Nigga! What you mean? Are you freakin serious? I keep this house clean every day, Nigga! So I'm going to need you to miss me with that one for real."

"Oh really? It smells like a diaper sweat shop in this MF yo! You have diapers under the couch, on the side of the toilet, on the sink. Pick those MF's up and throw them in the trash! Damn!"

"Ok Jermaine, I'm not about to go there with you. Wow, can't you understand that I be tired?"

Juanita looked at him in anger and hurt pride. But Jermaine was hurt as well.

"Yes I do, but you're not that damn tired that you can't get up and throw away these diapers scattered around the house. Man, it stinks in here really bad."

You see, it was the little things like that, that eventually grew into bigger things throughout their marriage. But eventually they got their priorities together some what, when they started taking church more seriously.

As their family grew from two children to nine kids, Things got a little bit crazy. It was to the point that they hardly had any time for themselves. Unless they were having sex.

Other than that, Jermaine was always working, or making money selling and breeding dogs. Or doing spoken word for some convention or church. While Juanita was doing hair at the shop, or singing for the church, or at someone else's church singing for them.

You would ask yourself, where are all the children at during any of this? They were right there along with them, or Juanita's parents were watching over them. Sometimes they were stuck at home by themselves. But most times they were at their grandparent's house daily.

During the time, the coming of these children were planned, but it was bad timing. Juanita and Jermaine were mentally and physically abusing each other. And each time they came back together, it was some explosive make up work done, that brought a baby into the picture.

They would totally forget that they were Christians, while in that mode of making love. Hair would be pulled, names would be called out, panties were getting ripped off. But they didn't care. They were married, and had the attitude that anything goes. Until one day, something big broke out.

"Juanita would you just shut the hell up and listen for a moment?!"

Jermaine shouted at her one day, steaming that she was trying to talk over him.

"Ok Juanita, can I talk now?!"

"Go ahead, nigga!" Juanita shouted back at him.

"Like I said, the people of the church does not come before your family. You take care of home first."

"I am taking care of my home!" Juanita barked at him. "You just want me here to have sex all day."

"Are you serous, yo?" Jermaine grew even more outraged at her. "You half cooking meals, I'm cleaning and washing the kids clothes by myself now, and getting them ready for school. All so you can sing for these niggaz! They should understand that you have a family. They ain't paying you to sing."

Jermaine let out all the frustration he'd been holding in.

"And you're barely making any money at the shop. You're barely making any money to pay your booth rent, or the products you're using on your clients."

"So you want to throw that in my face now, nigga?" Juanita sneered back at him.

"What I'm saying is you're giving them too much of your time. And they're not God, so quit trying to use God to justify the fact that you don't want to be at home, and you're having fun doing you without a care in the world."

Jermaine finally told her what he felt deep inside. That she didn't want to be there.

"Whatever, Jermaine."

Juanita dismissed the conversation with a wave of her hand.

Eventually, Jermaine left the church and started attending service elsewhere. The seed of division was already planted. He started working overtime just to avoid being at home, and to get away from the arguments.

Chapter three

One week, all the arguing and chasing stopped.

"I'm about to go braid this girl hair, Jermaine." Juanita said to him curtly.

It was already 5pm in the evening when she decided to go braid some girl's hair.

"Ok, cool." Jermaine responded. He didn't think nothing of Juanita doing anything due to she was never the type to wander off into anything.

Juanita left and went off, jumped into her car with all her hair material and sped off.

Time proceeded to go by, and it was dark outside. Jermaine started to worry, to the point he began to call.

'I wonder why she's not answering her phone?' Jermaine thought to himself, when it kept going to voicemail. 'This isn't like her at all.'

Moments later, she decided to call back.

"What you want?" Juanita's voice was impatient and rude. "I seen you blowin up my phone."

"Where you at?" Jermaine asked her.

"Ugggh, none of your business." Juanita snapped back.

"What the hell do you mean none of my business?! You've been gone since five o'clock and it's now after twelve midnight!"

"Well I'm at the bar with an old friend."

What was crazy, was that Jermaine already knew it was a guy. Because weeks before, people had informed him that they'd seen his wife hanging around some dude.

Juanita didn't return home until after seven am that morning, right on time for the kids to be sent off to school. This was now going on for weeks at a time. Until one day, while Juanita was sleeping, Jermaine went off into her phone, and saw the back and forth texts between her and a guy named Gully money rags.

Jermaine thought to himself, 'really? What kind of name is that?'

He looked the guy up on Facebook and saw what he looked like, after reading the texts. He then woke her up with a smack to the head with her own phone.

"B$***! What is this? So now you cheating?!"
Jermaine shouted at her; he was in a rage.

"Give me my God damn phone!" Juanita jumped up, pissed off. "That's what you get, going off into my phone. I'm about to call my daddy and tell him to come get me!"

But in the process of her calling her father, she also called Gully. Now Gully and Jermaine are arguing on the phone and going back and forth.

Juanita interrupted, shouting at Jermaine.

"Jermaine, look! I'm sucking Gully up now, nigga. And doing a good job at it. Our time is up."

Juanita had no heart at all when saying this. It was the most low, degrading, savage mind thinking, and epic thing ever thrown in Jermaine's face.

Jermaine was furious and heartbroken. The first thing that crossed his mind was to kill her.

"Oh really, hoe? So this is what we do? You just going to cut off into me cold hearted like that?"

"I just thought I'd let you know." Juanita said dismissively.

"We been together eleven years, and this is how you want to go out, b$***!" Jermaine was boiling. But Gully suddenly spoke into the phone.

"Yeah nigga, you miss the spaghetti and tilapia, huh nigga?" While Juanita was in the background giggling.

For weeks after that, Jermaine kept getting blocked calls from Gully, threatening him. And Juanita saying little things to him that would tear into him mentally.

He started smoking cigarettes and drinking, he completely threw God on the back of the bus. Jermaine was really frustrated and confused. . Looking at everything that had taken place, and what they'd built over the years, go down the drain.

The thoughts ran through his mind and caused havoc on his senses.

'Oh damn, what's going on? How did the devil slip in so easy? Letting others who had their own opinions come in with their dysfunctional relationships. We let them intervene.'

Jermaine was driving around full of crazed thoughts, feeling dumb, with a 38 in the back of his trunk, not thinking straight.

What if the cops pulled him over? And now the passenger, which was his homeboy and didn't know about it, would probably go down with him.

"Nigga you trippin! Let her ass go! Screw that nigga, man it ain't worth it." His boy Brandon said to him in the car.

Brandon was a shorty, with the mind of a hustla. He could hustle anything, but mainly thought with his other head. He kept Jermaine's mind on rapping and females, getting money than anything else.

"You right." Jermaine replied. "This mess is driving me crazy. I guess I'll...well we'll head to the poetry lounge."

The poetry lounge was a place Brandon introduced Jermaine to. It allowed him to blow off steam with the spoken word.

They went there every Wednesday night, until that no longer was an escape for Jermaine, because Juanita and Gully became worse. So to avoid the situation getting any more dangerous, Jermaine moved onto another city which was two hours away to find himself.

Part two

Getting it In

Chapter Four

"I feel so bad, grandma. I feel like I lost everything. My house, my cars, my job, my mind. I can't even think straight."

Jermaine sat and spoke to his grandmother one day, pouring his heart out to the one person that would listen. She responded to him with wisdom and understanding.

"Baby, God allows things to happen for a reason. You and Juanita wouldn't listen! Yaw did what you all wanted to do."

Grandmother Jean spoke the words he knew to be true.

"I know," Jermaine said sullenly. "But we still went to church. It was just certain things Juanita didn't want to listen to."

"That's only because she kept getting her family involved, and not God." Grandmother Jean replied. "You've gotten so small!"

His grandmother fussed over his extreme loss of weight in concern.

"I know, that's from me stressing grandma."

"Well we've got to feed you and get you back to being healthy. You've given that girl too much power, and don't no man or woman supposed to have that type of power, but God."

"I know, grandma...I know."

From weeks to within a month, Jermaine picked back up his normal body weight. He wasn't off into church as much as he once was, but he was going. He was still stressed due to the fact that his family was broken up.

One day, Jermaine was gathered around his people, who just so happened to bring up the past.

"My nigga, whatever happened to that one chick that used to be at Auntie house on 25th street, back in the day?" Said his cousin, Key.

"Man, I don't know. But I still think about her." Replied Eric.

Everyone was continuing to enjoy each other, due to not seeing one another in years.

"Jermaine, you remember back in the day, when Auntie had to come get you at Tamar's house, when you all got caught doing it?" Eric blurted out, and everyone started laughing.

"Man, that was devastating." Jermaine chuckled. "I'll never forget that."

"Yeah, I heard she ended up pregnant too." Said Key, looking at him curiously.

"I heard something about that, too." Eric jumped in. "But don't nobody know where Tamar is. It's been years since anyone's seen her. You know she was never stable."

"Man, my girl is cool with Tamar on Facebook, hold up. Jennifer, come here!" Key yelled into the house. Jennifer stuck her head out the door.

"What's up?" Jennifer asked him.

"You friends with Tam ass on Facebook, right? What's her last name?"

Jennifer responded with a shrug.

"Tamar crud."

Jermaine looked her up immediately, due to it's been 17 years since he's seen her. He left her a message in her DM.

He said to her: 'Hey you, you probably don't remember me, it's been a while. I'm hoping to hear from you soon. Blessings.'

Then he cut his phone off, sat back and thought about her. 'Damn, 17 years.....'

Two weeks later he was on Facebook, and just so happens to see that she wrote back. She had written him close to a week ago, and it said: 'Yes, I remember. It has been a long time. I started to call you, but you never responded to my message. Get back to me.' Jermaine immediately wrote her back. Moments later, Tamar called him.

"Wow, hey stranger. It's been a while." Jermaine said with pleasure.

"Yeah, I know." Tamar replied.

They both talked for hours, catching up from 17 years. Chatting from after 9pm till 1 am in the morning. Suddenly Jermaine changed the tone of the conversation.

"There's something I've always wanted to tell you, Tamar"

"What?" Tamar asked, curious.

"I've always loved you. Always. And just to inform you, you were my first."

"Oh wow, really? I wouldn't've been able to tell." Tamar said, with a smile in her voice.

"Well since we're revealing secrets to one another, I have one as well." She said to him.

"Really?" It was Jermaine's turn to be curious.

"Yeah, I do." Tamar replied. "Well just to let you know, when you left, I ended up pregnant."

Jermaine paused and went into silence.

"By the way, I do have your daughter." Said Tamar.

"Are you serious?" Jermaine was in shock. But Tamar responded with confidence.

"Yes, come to my job tomorrow at Walmart, and I'll show you a picture of her."

"What time?"

"Noon." Tamar replied.

That whole night till the late morning, Jermaine couldn't sleep. Knowing his first daughter, was by his first love. He couldn't wait until later on in the day to go to Tamar's job, and see her for the first time. And get this picture of his new daughter.

Chapter Five

Noon had finally came, Jermaine showed up and started looking around for Tamar, not knowing she had already spotted him the very second he came through the door.

Jermaine turned to the side and looked up, and there she was. With tears in her eyes.

"Oh my god! You still look the same!" Tamar said in surprise. "Can I get a hug?"

Jermaine smiled and reached out to hug her. He said, "Oh my," but in his mind he was thinking, 'damn she still thick, but even thicker now!'

All kind of lustful thoughts just ran straight through his mind. Tamar asked to see some pics of his kids. So Jermaine opened his phone up to show some photos of his son. Immediately, Tamar started crying and pulled out the photo of her daughter.

Jermaine's mouth dropped because the two favored him so much. You would have thought they had the same mother.

"So when can I meet her?" Jermaine asked.

"We're going to have to set up something, because she doesn't have a clue." Tamar replied. "This is going to confuse everything she's ever known."

They talked and talked, trying to figure out how to tell his child.

"What's her name?" Jermaine wanted to know.

"Her name is De'dra." Tamar responded.

Several weeks had gone by, until the day had finally presented itself. Tamar pulled up to Jermaine's house with De'dra.

She got out of the car with her little mickey mouse glasses on, looking around curiously. Not having a clue she was about to meet her father for the first time.

They sat outside due to it was a sunny day out. The young girl was sort of in shock and amazed at her surroundings, not knowing that the brick house she rode past every day, that she'd marveled at for years, was her grandmother's house.

"Hey, how you doing?" Jermaine addressed Tamar. She replied back quickly.

"I'm ok. I see the sun has finally come out. It is a bit dry and muggy out today, due to the rain." She was nervously making small talk.

Jermaine decided to break the ice.

"So who is this?" He asked, looking at the young girl at her side.

"This is my daughter, De'dra." Tamar replied.

"What's good, Ma." Jermaine spoke to De'dra with a friendly smile.

De'dra smiled back and spoke up for the first time.

"Man, this house is nice."

"Thank you, it's my family's house. We've been here for years ever since I was eight years old."

"Wow." De'dra's eyes was shocked.

"Would you like a tour around the yard?" Jermaine was eager to show her around his home.

"Sure." De'dra smiled.

As they got up, he started to head towards the back of the house, where he would show them the gym and the boat they had out back.

"You guys have a lot of land. I'm surprised you don't have a pool." De'dra exclaimed in awe.

"We started to get one, but hey, maybe one day we will." Jermaine replied.

Tamar looked at De'dra, then looked back at Jermaine in contemplation. 'Well here goes nothing.' She thought to herself.

"De'dra, I have some news I need to tell you."

De'dra's eyes held a sudden caution in them.

"Momma, is it bad?" She asked in fear.

"Yes and no." Tamar responded earnestly.

"Who died?!" De'dra's face began to scrunch up in pain, thinking the worst.

"No one died, girl." Tamar assured her.

"Well I need you to listen closely, okay? Do you remember we had you and your little brother years back, have your mouth swabbed at court?"

"Yes." De'dra replied, curious now.

"Well that was a DNA test to determine if Eric was the father of you two."

"Momma, what are you saying?" De'dra was confused.

"What I'm saying baby, is that Eric is the father of Eli, your brother. But he isn't your father, sweety." Tamar told her gently.

De'dra's whole face was stricken in surprise.

"Oh my god momma! Really?"

As she broke down into tears, she held onto her mother, sobbing and broken hearted.

Tamar hugged her daughter, crying as well. She kept repeating to her gently, and softly comforting her.

"I'm sorry baby. I'm so sorry."

De'dra wept for a few more moments. She felt as if everything she had known was erased. Finally she took a step back and wiped her eyes. Staring at her mother with a probing gaze.

"Momma, do you even know who my father is?"

Tamar responded without hesitation.

"Yes, baby." She looked at Jermaine, then looked back at her daughter.

"He's your father."

Chapter Six

De'dra simply stared at the stranger who now took on a new light in her eyes.

"Oh my god, momma." She couldn't believe it.

Jermaine took a few steps towards her and reached out his arms.

"Come here please." His voice was low, as he knew this was all a shock to her.

As De'dra slowly came over to him, Jermaine asked her to take off her shades, so he could see her eyes. Because by this time, she had put them back on.

Jermaine was taken back at the startling resemblance in her face.

"Oh my...you favor your brother a lot." He said gently. "You would be my first born baby. I've always sensed you existed, but never knew for sure. You have nine more siblings as well."

De'dra's eyes widened in amazement, knowing she was the oldest of all of them.

"Can I get a hug, baby?"

As De'dra hugged her new father, Tamar watched in the background, still in tears. They all headed back to the front of the house.

Six months had gone by, and Tamar and Jermaine were now a couple. Jermaine's divorce was finalized, and they decided they wanted to take their relationship to the next level. Especially after reuniting after 17 years.

They decided to get married, and everyone was excited, making plans for the big day. Everyone except for De'dra.

"Dad, I really don't think you should marry my mom." De'dra said to him in confidence one day.

"Why would you say that baby?" Jermaine asked, confused.

"Dad, she's crazy. Look at all the stupid arguments yaw been in. Second, just the things she do. She's crazy. I just think you shouldn't do it. However if you do....it's on you."

Jermaine thought about it for a second. Feeling a sudden hesitation. 'But it's the right thing to do.' He thought to himself.

'I love her enough to marry her. Maybe she'll change. Especially if God is off in it.'

Tamar had a friend that was coordinating the wedding. She was also one of the bridesmaids, named Kadisha.

Kadisha was this thick five two, brown skin, babyface bedroom eyes woman. She was very well put together, and about her business.

Her and Tamar were somewhat very close. To the point she let her coordinate her whole wedding.

"I see you have your colors and the type of flowers you want to put out. Those are nice." Said Kadisha, as Tamar was showing her everything she wanted in the wedding.

Jermaine walked into the room and saw all that was displayed.

"I'm loving the colors." He replied.

"Yaaaas." Kadisha responded, smiling at him.

"So you pick up your tux yet?" Tamar asked Jermaine, grinning as well.

"Oh yeah. I picked it up around 12 noon, so I'm all good." Jermaine replied with a smirk.

"Jermaine, does your tux match her dress?" Kadisha asked him.

"Yes, but my vest is burgundy on the inside. I'm a match with you all standing beside her."

"Okay." Kadisha replied.

Jermaine stooped over and whispered in Tamar's ear.

"I want Sadell to walk down the isle with your girl. We gotta hook them up."

Tamar shook her head and responded softly.

"Kadisha sort of out of his league."

"I was just saying, maybe she could calm him down. I feel she could be something different for him, other than the hood rats he's always attracting." Jermaine really wanted his boy to have better.

"I'll introduce them." Tamar finally agreed.

"Cool." Jermaine smiled in satisfaction.

Coming back from Walmart from picking up a few things for dinner a few days later, Jermaine and Tamar were in the car with the kids.

De'dra and Jay, Jermaine's son, were having a good time laughing and joking around. They were teasing Jermaine about eating so much sweets.

"Dad, all you eat is donuts and drink pop." De'dra chuckled.

"Yeah, you do dad." Jay agreed.

"So don't worry about what I eat." Jermaine replied in a joking manner.

However, Tamar was driving and laughing her head off. Agreeing to everything that the children were saying. Sipping on her energy drink.

"Let me get a sip of that." Jermaine said grumpily, reaching for the drink. But Tamar moved it out of reach.

"You better drink out of your own can." She laughed. "Why you want to drink up mine when you have your own?"

"Fine, I'll drink my own. But you act like I don't share with you." Jermaine replied, laughing as well.

"Man, I ought to pour half of mine in your lap to cool you off." Tamar was in hysterics, as she flicked water off of the cool can into Jermaine's eye.

"Awwe baby you know I can barely see!" Jermaine chortled as he reached for another donut. He grabbed his energy drink from the floor still dripping from the cooler, which he got it from in the store.

He looked over at Tamar and flicked some of the water off into her face. Two tear drops of it fell onto her sweat pants, and immediately, she flipped over all of the donuts onto the floor off his lap.

"Nigga! I don't play like that!" She yelled out at him. Anger radiating from her body.

Jermaine sat for a moment in pure shock. He couldn't believe she was serious. The children in the back were stunned into silence as well.

"Are you serious?" Jermaine asked, dumbfounded. "Why would you knock all of my donuts onto the floor?

Jermaine bit down on his lip, trying to remain calm. 'Wow.' He thought to himself. 'This was different.' He looked into the backseat at the kids, and De'dra looked back at him solemnly, with a telling gaze in her eyes. As if she was saying, 'I told you so.'

"What the hell you looking at her for?!" Tamar shouted at him.

Jermaine turned around and tried to regain his composure before speaking.

"I'm trying to figure out what just happened. One minute we was all enjoying one another with jokes. And the next, it's this B.S. right here."

Chapter Seven

As they drove up the street headed for home, this was a red flag that Jermaine knew he shouldn't ignore. But like most people do in these situations, when you love someone that much, you figure it'll change. And if not, you possibly could do something to change it.

Meanwhile, Sadell and Kadisha was getting to know one another. Kadisha had been inviting him to parties, and showing Sadell something other than the block. Which was what he was used to.

Sadell was more off into that thug life. But he was trying to find his way into a better one. However, for him it was a constant struggle.

Kadisha was considered a P.K. Which was preacher's kid. She went through college, and was on the sorority squad. She was even starting her own business.

She hung out with Sadell to get to know him, concerning the wedding. However, she did have a thing for bad boys as well. But like most girls of her status, she could only see Sadell as a friend. Which is what she explained to Jermaine and

Tamar, who had really thought they'd hit it off.

"Besides, I've seen a side of Sadell which I don't think I could tolerate." Said Kadisha, while sitting in their living room talking to Tamar about the situation that occurred between her and Sadell.

A few nights later, Jermaine came home from work.

"What a long day it's been." Jermaine sighed as Tamar sat up in the bed in boy shorts, looking all seductive.

"Shut the door." She replied, as he walked into the bedroom. "Did you get my messages?"

"No, I didn't." Jermaine responded to her.

"Well I've been watching porn all day, so you already know what it is that I want."

Tamar began to crawl across the bed to Jermaine, unbuckling his pants.

"I know what you like." She whispered.

"Tell me what I like." Jermaine replied back, aroused now.

Tamar looked up at him, as he stared down at her.

I'd rather show you." Tamar said sensuously. She then inserted his soul into her mouth. French kissing his bottomless pit with the sweetest spit, that fell from her jaws like a fountain.

Love in the mid-evening was something that Jermaine's body had been grieving, and Tamar knew exactly what he wanted. They gave love making a new meaning.

They laid in one another's wet spots, drifting into the cold wind that blew in from the window fan.

You see, Tamar was nasty. She was what you called a freak. They would make love and have sex almost two to three times a day, seven days a week.

She would do it anywhere and anytime. And take it anywhere in her body. It was like whenever it came down to them getting down with one another, she would turn totally into a different person. A straight porn star. Which drove Jermaine crazy in the heat of the moment.

But Tamar also loved to drink and smoke her Newports. Which also influenced Jermaine to go off even more. Even though he'd already picked it up from his last wife, Juanita.

A lot of Tamar and Jermaine's arguments occurred when she was intoxicated. Tamar always said she could handle her liquor, however, she never showed it.

Either she wanted to get loud and fight and cry, or turn into some sex demon, that would drain him dry before sunrise. And even when the sun came up, Tamar would still be pouncing him out of his sleep. She was a freak come true, for Jermaine.

The big day had finally arrived, and everyone was in place.

"Man, I can't believe I'm about to do this again." Said Jermaine.

"I can't believe you are, too." Replied Eric.

The church was now packed, while everyone waited for the bride to come down the aisle. There were beautiful fall colors everywhere.

Everyone stood to their feet, as Tamar began to walk down the aisle. She had tears in her eyes, with the biggest smile on her face.

After the pastor said his words, they spoke their vows which were written out from their hearts. Then the pastor spoke again, saying the final words.

"By the power invested in me, I now pronounce you husband and wife. You may kiss your bride."

Tamar handed the bouquet to Kadisha, as she leaned over and kissed the groom, for about a good seven seconds deep.

The wedding party all walked off down the center aisle, to the hall of the church.

Everything began to move extremely fast, due to everyone wanted to party right after the dinner, and was headed to Kadisha's house. Where the reception was taking place.

After the dinner, Jermaine and Tamar headed home to change clothes, because it was about to be a lot of drinking and dancing that night. But in the process of changing, there were other things happening over the bathroom sink.

"Let's get one in before we head out." Tamar said breathlessly, already hot for him.

Jermaine was down for it, as he exposed himself and lifted up her dress from the back, as the water continued to run. Steaming up the sink mirror. This good, ten to fifteen minute quicky was all they needed, before they headed out to the reception.

They finally made it. The music was loud, all of their friends and family were there. Jermaine and Tamar were having a good time. Especially Tamar. Her cup stayed full. Jermaine didn't care too much for drinking, but this was a special occasion.

He was already drunk, and cameras were flashing all over the place. Then suddenly, the women all suggested that Tamar throw the bouquet. So Tamar went and stood in front of the garage door.

"One...two...three!"

Tamar counted, then released the bouquet.

The beautiful fall color flowers were tossed into the air. The women went crazy, as they scattered across the driveway to catch it.

Then out of the blue comes Kadisha over everyone, and possibly being the shortest woman there, snatches the bouquet out of the air.

"Oh my god!" Jermaine's sister, Teshawn replied. "Where in the world did you come from?"

The crowd went crazy as Kadisha exited the floor, with the biggest smile on her face.

"I'm a' save these." She stated with a grin. "God's going to bless me with a husband soon." She strutted off with the biggest faith bound heart in the world, turning up wine coolers and sitting off in the corner.

"You go, girl! You next!" Shouted Tamar.

Tamar was now Mrs. Taylor. Venturing off into another life that she'd never experienced before. She was so happy, especially during the honeymoon they'd taken in Vegas, and afterwards.

What could be better than two teenage lovers who'd finally found each other after seventeen years apart?

You would've thought that this story would have been a happily ever after type marriage.

But little did Jermaine know that there was a lot of mess that was bound to be uncovered, and discovered about the new woman in his life.

Part Three

Stay Woke

Chapter Eight

"Baby, I think we need to take God more seriously." Said Jermaine. "I'm a preacher now, and we got to set more of an example for our kids."

"I hear you baby. But it's not like I'm going to get this Christian thing overnight, damn." Tamar replied in agitation. "I don't need you judging me and on my back."

"Baby I'm not on your back. I'm just saying, I don't want to be a preacher in the pulpit. But people are seeing my wife buying a 5th at the store." Jermaine tried to reason with her.

"Nigga you smoke cigarettes too, Mr. Preacher man!"

"I know I do, which is why I said that we need to take God more seriously. I'm not judging you."

"Damn! You know what? These damn kids are too big for all the mess we be putting up with. You need to send they ass back to their mother if they wanna be nasty, and let them f$**k up her house!!" Tamar said with frustration.

"I feel you, and I'll talk to them, ok? Just chill out." Jermaine replied in exasperation.

Jermaine began to curse out his kids like crazy, feeling that his marriage was possibly on the line. He knew Tamar had no patience at all with kids. She always tried to get rid of her own child whenever she got frustrated. So Jermaine figured his children really didn't have a chance.

Moving from Saginaw Michigan, to Toledo Ohio, was a big move for them. Especially after the honeymoon. It seemed as if things were going good. But as soon as reality set in, things began to change for Jermaine and Tamar.

Jermaine's background was in the church, due to his grandparents. He had some street life as well, concerning his father and mother, but his grandparents he admired a lot. They instilled a lot of spiritual things within him. However, Tamar had no church upbringing whatsoever.

She had a pretty rough life. She'd had her first child at only twelve years old. which later on was given up for adoption. She'd never spoken of it again.

A lot of things had taken place in Tamar's life, which explained why she had such a high sex drive. Tamar was an evil freak who had two faces. You never knew what you were going to get. The very second your eyes opened in the morning; you could wake up to some nice soft oral drowning sex, or awaken to an evil wicked witch temperature on ten.

Tamar and Jermaine relocated after the marriage, but ended up moving back to where they had started. Mainly to help out with the family's church. It was one of the reasons why Tamar wanted to move back.

Tamar knew somewhat about God, and cried, wanting to be closer to Jermaine's family. Which she claimed she missed so much.

So Tamar found a job first while Jermaine stayed behind in Ohio, and until they found a house. Jermaine was sending money back and forth to Tamar to be saved. But the very second he finally came back together with Tamar, she had already hooked up with some old friends.

"Look Jermaine, I don't think this is going to continue to work." Tamar told him. "Because these kids just don't listen, and this church thing, I'm just not ready to face."

"Tamar really? It takes time. So what are you saying?" Jermaine looked at her for a long time.

"I'm saying I want a divorce. I'm just not going to stop drinking and smoking. Hell, you knew what I was about when you first got me. I'm a be me. Besides, I feel like I'm hindering you from your church thing."

Jermaine began to tear up, thinking to himself, here I go again.

All that fake bull crap Tamar had said, kicking and dogging his last wife. Saying how much of a blessing he was to her. Now she pulls this savage bull.

What was crazy, is that Tamar soon moved out and into the house she kept staying in, all the nights she would come home late from. Turned out to be her baby daddy's auntie.

This is what made it even more interesting, the guy she was cheating on him with, his brother stayed there as well, and was dating the auntie.

Tamar moved back into town to be with an old hit and run buddy, named Eric Buckley. Eric was about their age, in the mid thirties, but could pass for the late forties. He was a recovering alcoholic who smoked bud daily, played video games, and still lived with his parents.

Jermaine just couldn't understand what in the hell she'd seen in him. But clearly, it all came out. They had a lot in common, which was the alcohol and bud.

After the divorce, months had gone by, and you could see the tearing in on Tamar's skin. She started to actually look like who she was with.

Jermaine eventually met a girl named Kesha, who he hooked up with shortly after Tamar.

Kesha was in the medical field and worked as a nurse. She loved his children, and was also a freak in the bed. She was about her business and was a major upgrade from Tamar.

Till one day, Tamar decided to stop by while Kesha was at the home. There was a knock at the door.

"Come in!" Jermaine shouted out.

It was Tamar.

"I just stopped by to see how you was doing." Tamar said, coming into the house.

"I'm good." Jermaine replied, wondering what she really wanted. Tamar had no idea that Jermaine had someone new already, because she knew he loved her still.

"I know things ended sort of f$**ked up between us, but if you want to, why don't you come over later on tonight and we could watch a movie? I could cook some wings or something." Tamar smiled seductively.

"I'll see." Jermaine replied. "It depends on what time I get off work, I get out around ten. But I'll be out around that side of town around ten thirty.

"That's good. I'll be up." Tamar said. "I don't have to work."

"What yo man going to think about me coming over there?" Jermaine questioned her.

"I told you, he wasn't my man. And besides, let's not talk about that, okay? And I do want to talk to you about some things when you come over...if you come over."

Tamar walked off and strutted out the door, she looked back at Jermaine.

"I hope you make it over. Really." She said with a smirk.

"I told you, I'm a try." Jermaine replied and then closed the door.

Chapter Nine

That whole night that Jermaine was at work he was thinking, 'wow, if we get back together? I wonder what it is that she wants?'

Jermaine was totally forgetting all about Kesha, watching the clock as the time went down.

Waiting to punch out, he realized that he had to drop a friend off at home, first. Jermaine tried to be on his best behavior whenever he was around her.

Ms. Johnson.

Ms. Johnson was also a straight freak. She'd been after Jermaine ever since he'd started working at the Campbell's soup company. As a matter of fact, she was there three weeks after his divorce, comforting him through his pain.

On the weekends before work and after work. And even times on the way to work. Even while he was driving.

Ms. Johnson was pretty good at what she loved to do, when it came to pleasing. However every now and then, she would cross his mind on how she would suck the soul out of his body, on every chance she gets.

"What you got planned, Jermaine?" Ms. Johnson suddenly asked him, as they headed to his car.

"Well after I drop you off..." Jermaine hesitated to tell her what he was going to do.

"Drop me off and...?" Ms. Johnson probed him to continue.

Jermaine finally shrugged.

"Tamar wanted me to stop by for some wings..."

Ms. Johnson's eyes widened in outrage.

"Are you serious? After how that hoe dogged you? Now she wants to call you over for some wings? Don't be stupid, Jermaine." Ms. Johnson warned him. "She's playing you, I know, I'm a female."

"How you figure?" Jermaine replied back. A bit insulted. "I'm not saying you're wrong, but you know I still love her. And you know I'm not just going to up and be with her."

"What about Kesha?" Ms. Johnson asked the obvious.

"Ugggh! I know, right? But Kesha is still married." Jermaine responded. "And she's going through a divorce herself. Hell! She still stays with her husband during the process."

"You're in a whole bunch of mess." Ms. Johnson said, shaking her head. "Ever since your divorce you've been zoned out. It's almost like you totally forgot about God!"

"How you going to say I forgot about God?" Jermaine argued.

"Jermaine this chick is still married, not divorced." Ms. Johnson said, laying it out in the open.

Jermaine went off into silence.

"What are you all quiet for now? You know I'm right. You need to find God. I was just about to try to get me some from you, but it seems like you about to get you some tonight. Right along with a plate of fried chicken."

They both broke into laughter about it. But Jermaine was deep in thought.

"You know, you're right. I need to get myself together, especially by my grandparents depending on me falling in place, and possibly inheriting the church." Jermaine said quietly.

"Yeah, you don't want to be no fake pastor." Ms. Johnson replied.

"Riiiiight." Jermaine agreed. "I gotta get it together."

They finally pulled up to Ms. Johnson's home, and he dropped her off, and headed to his place. He called Tamar right away.

"Hey, I'll be over after I hit this shower."

"Okay, I'm waiting for you." She responded.

Jermaine put on her favorite cologne as soon as he stepped out the shower. He brushed his beard, oiled his body up and finished getting dressed. He then headed out the door.

Jermaine finally pulled up in front of Tamar's place, and knocked on the door. She answered it with her grey and scarlet robe on.

"Hey..." Tamar greeted him in a sultry voice.

"Hey." Jermaine replied back. He stepped in the doorway for the first time in the place she stayed.

They sat and laughed, talked about the past, and watched a few movies. Then suddenly Tamar turned to him.

"Okay, this is what I really wanted to talk to you about."

The music was playing silently in the background. (A religious love) by R. Kelly. Jermaine sat on the couch and listened, as Tamar began to pour her heart out in tears. Confessing everything and all she's done, and how she wants to make it work.

Then Tamar came out and said the words to him with a pleading gaze.

"I desperately want you to make love to me, Jermaine."

She stood up in Jermaine's face and pulled her robe off. And little did he know, as he silently prayed to God, she was wearing her Victoria secret see through night gown.

All Jermaine could see was nothing but her lower body, hips, Navel and thighs were in his face.

Tamar dropped to her knees while Jermaine sat there, speechless. She knew what he liked.

She started kissing down from his chest to his stomach, then unloosened his belt. Giving Jermaine straight eye contact as she whispered to him.

"Baby, I'm sorry. I love you."

She said the words just before she inserted his magic wand into her mouth.

Jermaine just sat there with his eyes rolled to the back of his head. Zoned out. Thinking to himself, 'what am I getting myself into? Why am I here?'

The night turned into a sex crave. Jermaine pounded her out from one end of the couch to the other. They made love several times that night. Until they'd exhausted one another. It was like making love for the first time. They couldn't get enough of each other.

They laid naked on the couch until the early morning.

Chapter Ten

As time proceeded to take its course, Kesha left off with a broken heart. Besides, she was still married, but eventually got her divorce. She later on ended up with a white boy.

Kesha was a beautiful girl, however Jermaine couldn't see her value due to the fact that he was still in love with Tamar. Which is why he gave her a second chance.

Months went by, and Jermaine and Tamar were getting closer than ever. It was almost like they had never broken up. Jermaine was back to taking her out, cooking her dinner, buying her things, he was all the way in love with her.

"Baby, we should sneak off to Vegas and just get married again." Jermaine said to her one day.

"I agree, baby. But this time, we don't need everybody knowing." Tamar replied to him. "We're going to do this our own way."

"Okay, baby." Jermaine agreed.

Things couldn't get better. Till one day, Jermaine came home from work, and Tamar called him and left him a voicemail saying she was going to be at the carnival.

"I'm not home Jermaine, I'm at the carnival with a friend. I'll call you when I get home." Tamar said to him in the message.

Jermaine wanted to know who she was with. He sent her a text.

'Who you go with?' He texted her.

'Eric.' Tamar replied back through text.

Jermaine hit the roof. He sent her a series of angry responses.

'Eric? Are you serious? The same guy you cheated on me with?'

'Me and him will always be friends, Jermaine.' Tamar texted him back. 'Besides me and you aren't together, we're not married.'

'I know we're not married, but damn, I wouldn't put you in that position!' Jermaine was furious.

'I gotta go, I'm not about to do this right now with you, and I have these kids with me.' Tamar sent a final text then left.

Right then and there, Jermaine should have taken heed to the huge red flags, because from that moment on, she stopped responding to his texts. She began telling him she wasn't coming home at certain times no more. It was always, 'I'll let you know when I'll be home.'

There were a lot of times she spent with eric, for them to just be friends. It was as if everything was happening all over again.

"Tamar, do you seriously love me?" Jermaine asked her one night.

"Nigga, why you keep asking me the same questions all the time?" Tamar replied impatiently.

"Because love don't make you feel this way." Jermaine responded.

"Well you can feel free to walk away anytime, if you feel like it." Tamar told him dismissively.

"Damn! It's that easy, Tamar?" Jermaine was hurt.

"Man, it's like little by little, I find myself falling out of love with you. But I am in love with you." Tamar said in agitation.

"That don't make no damn sense!" Jermaine shouted at her, as he watched Tamar begin to roll up a blunt. Which was something she'd picked up during their absence. Jermaine had also started smoking right along with her. Which he'd thought would truly win her back. But apparently it didn't.

Now he was even more off into sin. He found himself digging back into a grave he was once delivered from.

Things started to get really heavy. Jermaine and Tamar started to once again grow distant. She no longer wanted to have sex with him. And she started including her friends in on their business.

Tamar had a close friend by the name of Sabrina, who was supposed to have been a minister. Common sense would make you believe she'd lead her in the right direction one day. Until one afternoon, that outlook changed.

"Jermaine you vent to the wrong people." Sabrina said to him one afternoon. "How are you going to talk to Tamar's friends, about Tamar, and she's supposed to be your wife? Well was your wife."

"Are you serious?" Jermaine asked her. "Any other time she never cared about me talking to her friends, and most times she was with me when I did. I don't want her friends."

"But what does the bible say, Jermaine?" Sabrina pressed him.

"Cling to your wife." Jermaine replied. "You're right. Then you should've told her to cling onto me as well, right? What did you tell her about cheating on me?"

Sabrina got silent.

"How can you tell me about God, and point out my faults, when you're caught up in fornication too, about to sit here and roll up a blunt."

Jermaine cut her down instantly.

"You sitting here talking about marrying people and building a ministry, yet you're high as hell, taking up for your friend. Right is right, wrong is wrong, so don't preach to me about God. I know the word."

Tamar sat there across from him on the couch with her friend, with an evil look on her face. If looks could kill, Jermaine would have died right there in the living room.

"Okay you can go now." Tamar said to him coldly. "Come back later, or not at all."

Tamar had totally changed. It was like Jermaine was standing in front of a different person.

Just months ago, she had stood in front of him, crying for another chance. Now she was pushing him away again. And Jermaine began to become bitter and angry.

So he left and jumped into his car, and pulled off.

Part Four

Starting Over

Chapter Eleven

Jermaine was on the phone with his boy Brandon.

"Bro, this broad is back on that B.S. again." He complained, trying to find solace.

"Bro, I keep telling you to forget that hoe. She was not the one for you. Man, you need that type of woman that's on the same page as you." Brandon said to him. "You should've just banged her out, got sucked up, and moved on and took care of your daughter. And did the same thing with Juanita. Because these hoes don't want to be saved, man."

"I know, right?" Jermaine replied, knowing his boy spoke the truth. "Man, all the stuff I've done for her just went up in flames. This chick has no compassion at all. All she wants to do is suck, and get bent over, and spark up."

"You out of place, man. You need to find God again, nigga. You've outgrown these hoes you've grown to love."

"I guess if you say so. I just thought she would change. And I actually prayed God a send this hoe back to me."

"Man, God sometimes a give you what you want, just to show you it wasn't what you really needed." Brandon said to him wisely.

"I totally agree." Jermaine nodded his head while holding the phone. "I don't know why I dumb down myself to some of these women that need all of this fixing. Man, she didn't even really want to deal with my kids. Or hell, even deal with her own. So I know my kids didn't have a chance."

"Nigga that should have told you something then, when she tried to give her son away." Brandon said with disgust.

They continued to talk on several other things as well, as Jermaine vented to his friend. But it wasn't enough of an outlet. Soon, he began to post things on social media, saying things that was way out of pocket.

Then one day, Jermaine got a message on Facebook saying, 'this doesn't sound like the Jermaine I met three years ago. What's going on with you? What happened to that Godly man?'

Jermaine quickly responded. 'He still here. I'm only human.'

Not really knowing who he was talking to, Jermaine went to the person's profile on Facebook. And that's when he realized, it was Kadisha. He then continued the conversation.

'Yeah yo girl is some savage stuff. I'm so done.' Jermaine messaged her.

'Awwe, yaw were the cutest couple. I thought you both were working it out.' Kadisha replied back.

'I did too. But I guess she still has a lot of hoe left off in her. What was I thinking?'

'Well you know what, Jermaine? Fall back. Allow her to miss you. Start dating other people. You know, not sexing them, but date. Why don't you come up to my restaurant and try some of my food? You know I got a restaurant, right?'

'No I didn't. But I'm so ahead you. I've already started dating other people. This one chick is supposed to meet up with me this weekend from New York. But I'm a stop by and see you. Maybe tomorrow.'

'Ok cool. But try not to call, or even text Tamar. Give her some space. And you do you. And things might work out for you. However until then, see you hopefully tomorrow.'

And then she signed off.

The very next day Jermaine went up to visit Kadisha's restaurant, with his son to try some of her food. It was something different. It was African food, and it was delicious.

"Are you excited to go on your date?" Kadisha asked him.

"What date?" Jermaine replied.

"Didn't you say you had a girl coming from New York, here to visit you?"

"Oh yeah, but I wouldn't say it was a date." Jermaine replied with a shrug.

"Well let me know how it goes." Kadisha replied.

As they walked out the door of the restaurant, they continued to talk about their conversation. The level of their vibe just got heavy. She was mainly trying to redirect him towards God, and getting his life straightened out. Then just maybe God a send that special woman into his life.

"Jermaine, God don't bless mess. Just pray for Tamar, if you want her back." Said Kadisha.

"No! Hell no! I don't want her anymore. I'm a just chill, that's it. And enjoy life." Jermaine was adamant about that.

Jermaine eventually went on the date that weekend, and it wasn't what he expected. The first impression the woman gave to him, was sex. She came to the door with a blanket wrapped around her, butt naked. Jermaine came up with an excuse to just leave.

At that moment he knew what he wanted, and it wasn't Ms. New York. Even though he came close to asking her for some oral sex, due to how she put herself out there, on how good she give it, he just left. Then hopped on the phone with Kadisha to tell her how the date went.

Kadisha and Jermaine started hanging out a lot more, and talking about one another's past. Until one day, he ran up on Tamar.

"I gotta few things of yours that I want to give back to you. Do you mind if I bring them over?" Jermaine asked her.

"Yeah, bring it over now, it's cool." Tamar replied.

Jermaine had her things in the back of his trunk. He headed over to her house and knocked on the door. When Tamar finally answered it, little do you know, Eric was in the background on the couch, with his pajamas on.

"Oh my bad. I didn't know you had company. Oh wow. Can I get a cigarette?" Jermaine asked her, with a shuttered gaze.

Tamar handed him a square, and Jermaine walked over to the table to get a lighter.

"What's up, man?" Jermaine said to Eric.

Eric's head drops as he puts the cigarette that he'd already lit into his mouth.

"What's up." Eric finally replied back.

"Aye! Tamar let me holla at you a bit before I leave." Jermaine turned to her.

"I don't feel like talking right now, Jermaine." Said Tamar. She moved away from him.

"Nigga, she don't feel like talking." Eric said to him from the couch, looking at him with squinted eyes.

"Huh? What you say?!" Jermaine turned back to face Eric.

"I don't want no shit." Eric said to him.

"Yo! Tam tell your b$**h to fall back before I beat his ass." Jermaine was revved up.

"Ok Jermaine, it's time for you to go." Tamar replied quickly.

"You ain't gon' touch me." Eric threw back at Jermaine. Foolishly baiting him further.

"Yo! Nigga you say one more thing, I'm a beat yo shit into that couch over there! Shut the f$*k up nigga!" Jermaine was in a haze of fury, and he was ready.

Chapter Twelve

Things now were chaotic at the moment. Tamar was now trying to push Jermaine out of the door.

"Don't do this in my house!" Tamar shouted at him, while trying to shove him out.

"Then tell yo b$**h to shut the hell up!" Jermaine shouted back at her.

Eric was still mumbling mess under his breath. So instantly, Jermaine grabbed Tamar and pushed her out of the way, and grabbed Eric by the back of his neck.

"Nigga didn't I tell you to shut the hell up, or I was gon beat yo shit in, boy?" Jermaine said the words with a crazed look in his eyes, then tossed Eric onto the arm of the couch.

Tamar was going crazy.

"Jermaine get out of my house, you're not welcome here anymore! That was the last straw!" She yelled out at him.

"Well can I ask you one thing? Is it permanently over between us? No coming back?" Jermaine asked her.

"Hell yeah it's over, f$**k you!" Tamar shouted back at him, while Eric stood in the background on his phone like a lost nigga looking for a way out.

"So we single, and can talk to whoever?" Jermaine pressed further. He just wanted to hear her say it.

"I don't care who you talk to, just get out and don't come back." Tamar confirmed it for him.

Jermaine headed out, but before he did he looked back at Eric, and said one last thing to him.

"You a weak ass nigga."

"Go! You childish as f$**k!" Tamar shouted at him.

Jermaine turned back to her, with a fierce gaze.

"And you're what everyone told me you were...which is a savage hoe."

Then Jermaine walked out and got into his car and sped off.

When Jermaine got home he was still fuming over what happened earlier. His sons were concerned as they looked at him. They asked him what was going on.

Jermaine started to explain it all, at the same time laughing, because it had happened so fast. But like teenagers, they jumped on the phone and started asking and telling De'dra what happened, as if she already knew what their father had done.

But like all women, Tamar told De'dra something totally different. As if it was the truth, and Jermaine's story was made up. But deep down inside, Tamar knew her man had his tail tucked in between his legs.

Jermaine knew he was wrong, and that the situation could have been dealt with better than that. He didn't want to even tell Kadisha what had happened, so he called Ms. Johnson up. Knowing she would suck his sorrows away.

Jermaine started talking to himself, riding alone in his S.U.V. thinking 'damn, what has happened to me? I'm back to smoking weed, doing and thinking the worse things. This isn't me.' Jermaine thought to himself. 'Something's gotta give.'

So he finally went over to Kadisha's house, and explained to her all that had happened.

"Jermaine, nooo! You just showed her how pressed you were." Kadisha told him, shaking her head.

"But man, that nigga wouldn't shut up!" Jermaine grunted in frustration.

"Jermaine, you just let the devil win." Kadisha said quietly.

"I know." He replied to her.

"You gotta distance yourself from ever dealing with her, or she will continue to keep you going in a circle, chasing her. Just face the fact that she doesn't want you. Tamar was in love with the things you did for her, not you."

Jermaine began to realize that these were facts that Kadisha was spitting to him. He decided to just continue to date. However he spent a lot of time with Kadisha and her children. But throughout the months, they both realized they could never be, due to Kadisha was best friends with Tamar.

Until one night, Jermaine came over to discuss going on a date with someone he was meeting off Facebook, but it didn't fall through. So Kadisha suggested that he come with her to this party she was invited to, by an old friend.

"Jermaine, why don't you just go to this party with me? We don't have to stay long, and besides there's plenty of food there." Kadisha said to him. She knew Jermaine loved to eat, and that could be the only chance she had of getting him to come to the party with her.

I'll think about it. Besides, it sort of makes me uncomfortable going to house parties." Jermaine replied. "People die at house parties."

Kadisha laughed. "It ain't even that type of party." She chuckled.

As Jermaine procrastinated, the night faded out, and all they did was sit on their cell phones. And laugh and watch YouTube videos.

"Yo, you remember this song?" Jermaine asked her. Pulling it up on his cell phone. It was an old video on YouTube of Babyface. Kadisha smiled the very second he turned it up.

"Oh yeah, those were the days." Kadisha grinned. "When music was music. My mother didn't allow me to listen to it though, due to we was a church family."

"So you was a P.K." Said Jermaine, smiling at her.

"I guess you could say that." Kadisha laughed in reply. "But I know my music."

"Do you want to slow dance? Or should I say, can you slow dance?" Jermaine asked her.

"I can do a lil something. But I'm not too good." Kadisha responded.

As the music began to play, it drifted from (Rome) I belong to you, to (R. Kelly) feeling on your booty, and so forth. Things started to get heated between the two, and Jermaine started kissing Kadisha softly on the neck.

"What are you doing?" Kadisha asked breathlessly.

"I'm sorry." Jermaine replied, lifting his head. I got a little bit caught up in the moment."

"I'm just saying, we can't be doing that. Things can happen." Kadisha said to him.

"Things like what?" Jermaine wanted to know.

Kadisha smiled at him, and played stupid, continuing to dance with him, while trying to keep him at a safe distance.

"You can't be doing that." She said again softly, as Jermaine nibbled on her ear, and gently kissed along her neck.

"What can happen?" Jermaine asked her again, as he kissed her skin.

"Oh my, you playin..." Kadisha moaned softly.

Jermaine gently grabbed her fat booty and squeezed it tight. She inhaled deeply and moaned again.

"We can't be doing this."

"Doing what?" Jermaine teased her.

Chapter Thirteen

Jermaine gently patted and caressed her cookie through her leggings.

"Jermaine no...no Jermaine..." Kadisha's voice was shaky and aroused.

"Tell me to stop baby, and I'll stop." Jermaine said in Kadisha's ear.

"No, don't stop...don't stop..."

They both moved towards the couch, as Kadisha fell down on the arm of it. Jermaine slowly pulled down her pants and noticed that she had on boy shorts, which was such a turn on for him.

One thing led to another. Kisses and tight squeezes, licking and sucking to tongue teasing.

This right here, should have never taken place, however the sex is always the best, when it's not supposed to be happening. This was where you were supposed to draw the line. This was Tamar's best friend, but Tamar had left that door open, and it was not intentionally.

After counters and counters of sensational hot butt naked sex...

"Jermaine, we can't be doing this. What if Tamar finds out?" Kadisha said after they lay spent.

"So what if she finds out?" Jermaine shrugged it off.

"Did you do it to me just to get even with her?" Kadisha asked him quietly.

"No, it's nothing like that. So don't let this change our friendship." Jermaine replied.

"So what does this mean?" Kadisha questioned him, wanting to know.

"Let's just keep it friends." Jermaine said to her.

"I agree, Jermaine. But this can't keep happening. Cause I don't wanna be nobody's jump off."

"Man, stop. You're nobody's jump off, okay?" Jermaine shook his head.

He began to put on his pants and wipe his face, from all the sweat from a long night's work. They had awakened after each orgasm, only to go back at it. Jermaine could finally say to himself that she was actually compatible. She kept his soul pouch on E, and her juices stayed overflowing.

Jermaine headed home in deep thought, while Kadisha lay completely naked in bed, in deep thought as well. His thoughts ran through his head like crazy.

'Yo! I can't believe this just happened. I never would of thought of sleeping with Kadisha, and it was actually the bomb.' He thought to himself.

Jermaine used to fantasize himself with her, but had quickly thrown those thoughts out, because he never would of thought sleeping with Kadisha could ever happen.

He arrived home and jumped in the shower, washing himself up.

Shortly after getting in the bathroom, his son, Sencier came in and questioned him.

"Hey dad, I see you didn't come home last night." Sencier said to him.

"Yeah I fell asleep on Kadisha's couch last night. We got to talking and watching movies, and I just found myself passed out." Jermaine said smoothly.

"You mean Tamar's Kadisha? Her BF? Dad, wow." Sencier just shook his head.

"Nothing happened, man." Jermaine lied quickly. He was talking to Sencier while in the shower, so it was easier to spin the tale.

"I know you, dad." His other son, Jay, replied. Having entered the bathroom as well.

"What you mean you know me?" Jermaine grumbled, while lathering the soap.

"Dad I know you. Kadisha has that big ole donkey booty, and those eyes, and she is just your type. The one I know you'll get down with." Jay said with confidence.

Both of his boys laughed behind the bathroom door, while Jermaine continued to shower.

Later on that day, Kadisha called Jermaine explaining to him that all of what had happened was a mistake, and that they should still date other people, and shouldn't allow the sex to change anything. So she continued to keep in contact with her male friend, Gary. And Jermaine was okay with that, due to he had a lot on his mind anyway.

Jermaine was preparing his son for his first prom and getting himself together for the ministry, with his grandfather's church. Because he knew he couldn't live both lives, and as for now, that's exactly what was happening.

Part Five

The Cake Lady

Chapter Fourteen

"Hey grandma, how you doing?" Jermaine was talking to his grandmother on the phone. It's been a while since he'd chatted with her.

"I'm doing okay baby, what's up?"

"I just need prayer, I have so much going on, and I'm confused." Jermaine replied in confidence.

"Well you just need to settle yourself down. You're trying to do God's job, he knows your needs and wants. If you just keep him first, Jermaine, and stand still and let him direct you, you'll be fine."

"I'm trying to, but it's so much pressure." Jermaine said in frustration. "But I understand what you're saying grandma."

"You don't only represent us, you represent God. People are watching you, and I know you don't want to make your grandfather ashamed. You're like his only son, basically, and we see so much potential in you. You'll come around, I trust God will make things right for you." His grandmother assured him with encouraging words.

"I receive that, grandma. I just need to get over the fact that Tamar did what she did, and was so cold hearted with it." Jermaine was still hurting from the fallout of events.

"We are all shocked, I didn't and couldn't see Tamar doing those things neither. But you chose her, not God, baby. God honored the fact that you got married and did right. However, that's what you wanted, not God." His grandmother spoke the truth.

That was real talk, that Jermaine's grandmother gave him. Even though at times it be somethings that he didn't want to hear. It was always right. She would never tell him nothing wrong. She knew his purpose, and knew the enemy was trying to distract him. She always told him that the devil was out to steal, kill, and destroy. And was using women to do it with Jermaine.

Jermaine needed a saved, sanctified woman, is what she kept telling him. His mother would tell him, the best way to get over someone, is to get under someone else.

And that's exactly what Jermaine had been doing. Until he met a chick named, Erica.

Erica pretty much was like a female version of him. Whomever Jermaine was stressed with, Erica was the one he would call. No matter what time of night it was.

She was a bit exotic. She would let Jermaine get it anywhere. Outside in the car, kitchen, bathroom, it didn't matter. They both was one another's stress relief. She was like a quick blunt, that adrenaline rush. She believed in Astrology though as heck, that their stars lined up on some planet Mars and stuff.

Then one day, Sencier approached him.

"Dad, Ms. Reeves wants to meet you." Sencier said to him.

"Who's that?" Jermaine questioned him.

"My prom date's mother. She seen you at the introduction at the assembly last week, when you came with Kadisha." His son responded.

"Oh well, for some odd reason I really don't remember her." Jermaine shrugged.

"Yeah, she was right next to you in line when we were leaving."

"Well find out what her Facebook page is, and I'll see what she looks like."

Moments later, Sencier finds out his prom date's mother's name is Karen Reeves.

Jermaine decided to message her to introduce himself, and she actually wrote him back within five minutes later.

She said that she'd like to meet him and chill and get to know him better. Jermaine responded, 'sure, just pick a date.' Due to the fact that he worked first shift, and would be home by three. But he indicated to her that he has Fridays off.

She replied back, 'cool. Well I'll hit you up on Friday.'

Jermaine soon started to remember who she was, by viewing her photos and thought to himself, 'okay damn, she a bit thick.'

And of course, when he spoke this unintentionally out loud, his son Sencier went and told his prom date what his father said about her mother.

At this point, Jermaine was actually feeling free. Kadisha and him viewed one another as friends. But continued to talk and socialize just as that. De'dra, Tamar and Jermaine's daughter started to fade away, due to the fact she started acted suspicious. As if she knew something was up between Kadisha and her father.

You see, De'dra looked at Kadisha like an Auntie. Especially by her and her mother Tamar being best friends. This is what made it sort of easy for Jermaine to walk away from Kadisha, due to the whole situation.

Then Friday approached, and Jermaine received a phone call from Ms. Reeves asking if he wanted to meet up that day, or later.

He replied, 'sure,' and then she asked where he stayed at.

"I stay on 149 Vestery drive." Jermaine gave out his address.

"Well I'll be over there around nine pm. When I finish doing my running around." She replied.

"Bet. I'll be here." Jermaine disconnected the call.

The day went by, food was eaten, and Jermaine's day couldn't get no better. Until nine pm hit, and a pretty little black KIA pulled up in front of the house.

"Dad, Ms. Reeves is here." Sencier said to him eagerly.

She stepped out of the car with these brown knee high boots, and grey leggings, with a tan sweater to match her brown M.C. purse.

"Hello, I'm Karen, the mother of Charity, the quiet girl your son's taking to the prom."

Jermaine was very pleased at the sight.

"Well hello, I'm Jermaine. Wow, you have a pretty big smile." Jermaine complimented her.

He watched her as she walked through the door of his home.

"Have a seat, would you like something to drink?" Jermaine asked her politely.

"Yes I would, do you have iced water?"

"Of course, I got you." Jermaine responded.

"By the way, you can call me Kay, instead of Karen, cause that's what I prefer."

"I got you, Kay." Jermaine smiled at her, and they both laughed.

Jermaine got the ice water and handed it to her.

"Do you smoke?" Kay asked him.

"No, I don't. But I used to. I smoke on cigarettes a bit when I'm bored or stressed." Jermaine replied.

"Well do you mind if I smoke?"

"Sure go ahead, because I gotta short anyway."

They both continued to smile at each other.

"Well I'm a put on this movie, it's pretty good." Said Jermaine, and Kay agreed. But they talked so much to the point that they didn't realize the movie was almost over.

Chapter Fifteen

Hours had passed by, and it was now one am in the morning. That's when Kay noticed her phone.

"Oh my god, my daughter's been blowing me up. And three movies done played and we just talked through both of them, And now this one." Kay shook her head and chuckled.

"Well I got to get home, you know. But I'll come through tomorrow and kick it with you, if you don't mind."

"You can do that, I'm cool with that." Jermaine replied, smiling.

Kay stopped and paused for a second, but then shook her head.

"Never mind, I was about to ask you something, but I don't want you thinking I'm some type of hoe or something." She explained.

"Keep it real, I won't think you're a hoe, what's good? We've already talked about almost everything for six hours straight." Jermaine reassured her.

"Well all night I've been wanting to ask you for a kiss, and I've been loving the way you been looking at me." Kay replied bashfully.

"Really? Well this is crazy. I'm a keep it real with you too. All night I been staring at your breasts wondering what it a feel like with one of them in my mouth?" Jermaine smirked.

Kay smiled back at him, and then leaned forward and kissed him. Deeply and passionately.

Kay had to be around four foot ten, she was a shorty who moved in big on things. Jermaine went from her lips down to her neck, and at that moment, somehow that breast fell out. And that led to it being sucked and kissed on. To the point her little knee high boots came off, then the leggings.

The situation was so tense, it was like it was something that they both needed and wanted from one another that night. Especially having some things in common like, screwed up relationships.

Kay's experience was that her husband of five years left her for a white girl. And had been cheating on her.

Both of them had been hurt, but perhaps this was just a way of them expressing what they had and shared in common.

The situation was weird due to Kay being so light and short. It was like handling a rag doll that fought back. Splash! Splash! Ripping her from the back, face deep off into the couch pillows, then finishing her off onto the floor.

It was now six am in the morning, and they were both just waking up.

"Oh my god, my kids get up in another hour. I gotta go, Can I come see you later?" Kay asked him, rushing with her clothes.

"Yes you can. I'll be here. Just get at me." Jermaine said to her.

As Kay hurried and threw on her clothes, she started to head out the door, but she turned and kissed him one last time.

A few moments later, Sencier walked into the living room.

"Dad, did Ms. Reeves just leave here?" Sencier asked him with a look.

"Yes she did." Jermaine replied with a smile.

"I don't even want to know." His son mumbled, as he turned to get dressed for school.

Jay was already gone, having left out the back door, due to the fact that he'd seen that Ms. Reeves was still there at the time. Due to seeing her car parked out front.

Later on that day, Ms. Reeves called Jermaine and asked him would he like to have dinner, if so bring the boys. And of course, he accepted. The boys were excited, but of course it made Sencier a bit uncomfortable due to the fact that he had a girlfriend. And that he was invited over to Charity's house, which was his prom date's mother, to have dinner.

"Do you all eat Ravioli?" Asked Ms. Reeves.

"Yes, we do." Jermaine replied.

"We eat anything." Jay responded as well. And thank you."

"Yeah, thank you." Sencier decided to remember his manners.

Kay fixed Jermaine's plate first, as he sat at the table with a glass of Kool-Aid. She served the rest, then finally sat down and joined them with a glass of wine.

"Would you like some wine?" She asked Jermaine.

"Sure, Ms. Reeves." Jermaine used formality in front of the kids.

"You don't have to call me Ms. Reeves." She chuckled. "The kids know I asked you to call me Kay."

"I got you, ma." Jermaine smiled. "By the way, the food is absolutely delicious." He complimented her, as the boys joined in and agreed.

A bit later, the boys went into the living room with Charity and her little brother, Jordan, and cousin Peaches.

Right then and there, it was obvious that a certain two had a little crush on each other. Which was between Jay and peaches. They clicked, but peaches was a little hood, and that was something Jay wasn't used to.

"You want some Patron?" Kay asked him.

"Just a bit, cause I'm not a drinker. But can I have one of your squares?" Jermaine replied.

"Sure, short me half on it." Kay responded.

As Jermaine sparked up the square, Kay proceeded to pour him a shot of Patron. They began to conversate.

"I gotta go to Lansing this week, well the outer skirts of it." Kay said to him.

"What for?" Jermaine wanted to know.

"I got family that lives there, and my mother had asked me to invite you, if you was up to it."

"What time and day?"

"Possibly the weekend, well tomorrow?" Said Kay.

They both started laughing. At that very moment, Kay had a little buzz. She was currently giving Jermaine a seductive look.

"Well we gonna have to get going cause we have church tomorrow morning." Jermaine mentioned, to stay focused.

"What church you go to?" Kay asked him.

Jermaine responded while putting his coat on.

"We go to, E.L.C. Eternal Life Center." It was once called Greater Faith Ministries.

"Okay." Kay replied. "Well I might pay you all a visit."

"That a be straight. I would like that."

The situation started to feel a bit weird due to Jermaine could see and feel that Kay was most definitely falling for him. But at the same time, he kept noticing how he was getting all these random text messages from Kadisha, that he kept ignoring.

Jermaine felt that messing with Kadisha was a no, no. And it couldn't go any further. And besides, Kadisha had agreed to it. Why not give Kay a try to see where their mysterious love was going to take flight to?

Chapter Sixteen

It had been a few days, more like a week, since he'd spoken to Kadisha. So he finally replied to one of her text messages.

'I'm assuming you must have found someone.' Kadisha had said in the message.

'I'm with a friend, that's it. Why you asking?' Jermaine replied back. And Kadisha responded.

'Because people are seeing you around town with this girl, all hugged up. And you just cut me and my kids completely off, but it's all good.'

'Kadisha you act like me and you was a couple. It wasn't nothing more, so why are you bugging?'

'Jermaine I'm just saying, but I don't care. I'll lose your number and delete all your pictures as well. You good, okay? Live your life.'

'Ain't that what I'm doing? At least that's what I thought.' Jermaine replied, frustrated.

'Nigga, I let you in with my kids and everything. But you good.' Kadisha texted back.

'Kadisha are you finished? I love your kids, tell them I said hi, okay? And I guess I'll see them around.'

'No I won't tell them hi, because that'll hurt them to find out I heard from you. They'll get over you.' Those were Kadisha's last words, and then she stopped responding.

On the way to Lansing, Jermaine experienced a weird moment.

"Wow dad, you and Ms. Reeves have really been into each other for almost two weeks now." Said his son Jay.

"I know, but she's something different. A bit weird, but something different." Jermaine replied.

Jermaine and his son Jay were the only two that went, while Sencier stayed back in town to work.

"Wow, this is a nice house." Said Jay, as they pulled up into the driveway.

"Damn, I know right?" Said Jermaine. They both got out the car and followed Kay and her children in through the garage, to the house.

"Hello." Said a darkskin beautiful, sweet woman. She had platinum grey hair, and was giving everyone a hug as they came in.

Jay looked at her with a shocked expression, like wow. "Hello." He responded back.

"There's plenty of food here for everyone to eat." The beautiful lady replied.

The woman, which was the mother to Kay, had prepared a huge feast, all for one night, in which they all were staying.

There was chicken, fish, spaghetti, salad, garlic bread, wine, and of course plenty of weed.

"So you're Jermaine. I've heard good things about you." Said Mrs. Williams, Kay's mother.

"And I heard good things about you as well." Jermaine replied back.

As he prepared for the evening dinner, Kay decided to give him a tour of the house. It was most definitely a beautiful home. Her mother actually worked out of the house. From the basement to the last floor, the place was definitely a dream house.

Jermaine came back upstairs from the basement, to where the children were all entertained at, and dinner.

After the meal, they all settled at the table smoking squares, while her mother rolled up a blunt.

"Wow." Jermaine turned towards Kay. "It's so funny how your mother's character is. She reminds me a lot of my mother, they would be the best of friends."

Kay's mother smiled at him, as they began to talk about what was interesting to Jermaine.

Kay got up and programmed the TV to the Christian channel, to an interesting minister that her and her mother admired. Jermaine looked around like, this is so weird, as he observed everything.

Blunts were being passed around the room, and glasses being filled with Cavosia, and Patron, while the minister was preaching on the TV. And at the same time, God was being discussed.

Her mother made it quite clear that all the males were to sleep downstairs, while the women would be upstairs.

It was getting close to the time they would turn in, and it was already after three am in the morning. Kay walked with Jermaine downstairs to the basement. She turned and gave him a kiss.

"I love you, goodnight." She whispered to him.

Jermaine paused like, woa she's really serious with this?

"I love you too." He replied back, as it seemed like the right thing to do in the moment. They kissed each other standing on the second to last stair, then she headed back upstairs.

Bleep, Bleep. It was another text message from Kadisha, that morning. 'Would you call me, please.' It said. But Jermaine kept ignoring it, because he didn't want to feel any type of way, about making him feel sorry for her. He felt he needed something else, and Tamar's friend wasn't it.

So to avoid the arguing with Kadisha, he'd rather not answer. Due to all the time Jermaine was spending with the cake lady.

That was the private nick name he'd given her. It definitely seemed to fit.

Part Six

No such thing as perfect

Chapter Seventeen

"Hey, it's been a long time, how are you?" Tamar called him on the phone one day.

"I'm doing pretty well." Jermaine replied.

"I heard that you and Kadisha was messing around at one point." Tamar inquired.

"We were." Jermaine responded. "But now we're just cool."

"I knew that b$**h wasn't really my friend!" She sucked her teeth and rolled her eyes.

"Whatever, Tam. Aren't you supposed to be happy with your bomb ass nigga?"

"I'm good." Tamar replied offhandedly. "Your daughter told me you have a new girlfriend, and she was cute."

"Well they say you're supposed to do better than your last, right?" Jermaine responded.

"If you say so." Tamar replied. "I didn't call you to argue with you, okay? I don't want to come between you and the cake lady." She started laughing, as it was now known what he called her. Jermaine jumped to his woman's defense.

"Well she has a dream and she has goals. And I know for a fact that she sees further than sitting on the front porch all summer, turning up, sleeping around with everyone's man."

"What the hell you mean?!" Tamar shouted, quickly taking the offensive.

"I'm not saying you do that, I'm just saying she's a lot different than most. Besides Kesha, that I dissed for your ass."

"Whatever." Tamar sucked her teeth again. "But I'm happy for you. I just thought you crossed the line screwing around with my best friend."

"Are you serious? Which was worse? You cheated on me while we were married. Do you honestly think I would have been with anyone else, especially your best friend, had you not cheated?" Jermaine flung back at her.

"Well, that's in the past."

Tamar didn't really want to go off into it because she knew Jermaine was right.

"I didn't intentionally try to dig off into your friend, straight up." He said earnestly.

"Well okay, Jermaine." Tamar replied. "It's just so weird that I dreamed you two were together years ago, and then it actually took place."

"But I'm not with your girl now, so your dream was nothing but a kitty nap, and a short illusion." Jermaine said.

"If you say so." Tamar grunted.

"So are you still seeking advice from your so called minster friend?" He probed her.

"You trying to be funny?

"I'm just saying." Jermaine shrugged. "She tried to come for me in defense for your ass, and spiritually have all these side blinded issues herself. That bothered the hell out of me. Like, seriously, how you gonna preach to me and tell me how wrong I am, but lost like hell yourself?"

"Why don't you tell her that yourself?" Tamar asked him.

"That ain't my friend, that's yours. I find it hilarious that she tried to come at me with the bible, and I shut her down that easy. She couldn't justify nothing that I was saying, straight facts. She should of seen herself at the same time she called herself trying to correct me."

Jermaine was on a roll, as he vented.

"She saw discord in so many ways, at the same time, she was so hypocritical in everything she threw at me."

"You're so judgmental." Tamar said, impatiently.

"No, I'm not. Put it this way...if you steal, would I be wrong to call you a thief? And if I lie consistently, would I be wrong to call you a liar? There's no justifying that, right?"

"How is the cake lady spiritual?" Tamar changed the subject and tried to direct it back to his woman.

"Her name is Karen, Kay for short." Jermaine corrected her. "And she understands. She has a church background. But we ain't perfect. But she's wise enough to not make the type of moves I've seen happen in my past."

"Why do yaw call her the cake lady? Is it because she's fat, or likes cake or something?" Tamar wanted to know and started laughing.

"You got jokes." Jermaine chuckled. "No, it's because she likes to bake. What does Eric do? Play video games and down coronas, and smoke blunts all day?"

"No, he has a job." Tamar replied sarcastically.

"But he still home bound with momma right? But stays with you on his days off." Jermaine was brutal, but didn't care at this point. "Go be with what you attract, and what you are. That's what you're used to,"

"Okay Jermaine, I gotta go."
Tamar hung up the phone in his ear.

The relationship between Tamar and Jermaine became bitter sweet, unlike Juanita and Jermaine. Juanita had two faces. One moment she was cool, the next she was wishy washy. Especially when she got a man.

Tamar and Juanita both had issues, when it came to men. The first sign of frustration, they were quick to open their legs to another. They say you can't turn a hoe into a house wife, well Jermaine was starting to believe that was the stone cold truth.

It was now going on four weeks between Kay and Jermaine's relationship, and it had grown stronger. However, there had been some craziness going on with Kay and her past relationship, and she decided to talk to him about it one day.

"Baby, we need to talk." Said Kay.

"Sure, what's going on?" Jermaine replied.

"Well my cousin keeps sending messages to me from my ex, and I keep telling him that it's over. And it's really starting to get frustrating."

"Well just tell him how it is, and if he doesn't like it, oh well." Jermaine shrugged.

"He's even talking about killing himself, and if me and you end up together, he'll never go away." Kay seemed frantic over this guy.

She pretty much painted a picture of her ex as a maniac. Well, sensitive maniac. Jermaine refused to speak negative things about him, due to he'd felt that pain before. But he did notice Kay was a bit drunk as well, during the conversation.

"Baby let's get out and go for a ride." Jermaine tried to distract her. Kay agreed.

So they drove through the streets in the late night, listening to music, as he serenaded her, singing along with the love songs programmed in his car.

They figured since they were out, they might as well get a bit to eat. So they headed to Applebee's and dined in for a while, before heading back to her place.

Chapter Eighteen

Pulling up to the driveway, all you could see is the biggest smile ever on Kay's face.

"Thank you for taking the stress away, I needed the talk. It cleared my mind." Said Kay, smiling.

"Anytime." Jermaine smiled back. "Well I gotta get home to these boys and make sure they get up for school tomorrow."

"You couldn't spend the night and just get the boys, and bring them over?" Asked Kay.

"Well if you want me to." Jermaine replied.

"Jermaine, I wouldn't suggest it if I didn't want you to." Kay responded.

So Jermaine headed to the house to pick up the boys, knowing that Jay wouldn't mind, due to he was fooling around with the niece. But Sencier was so in love with his girlfriend, he would just sit at home on the phone all night by himself.

Later on that night, Jermaine came out the shower and entered Kay's room with a towel around his waist. As she uncovered herself, exposing her red laced Victoria secret night wear. With a glass of wine poured for him on the side of the bed.

The cigarette was lit, as she closed the door and dimmed the lights, over her fireplace. The night was strong and long.

Later on that morning, he woke up to breakfast. French toast, eggs and sausage. And Kay was braiding hair.

The sun was out, but it was still cold as heck. Squares were being passed left and right. Jermaine became somewhat of a train smoker. He stared at Kay braiding up her friend's daughter's hair. Then all of a sudden, there was a knock on the door. Kay runs to go get it.

"It's here! It's here!" She shouted excitedly.

Jermaine walked over to the front counter to see what all the excitement was about.

Kay opened up a package that the mail center dropped off. She lifted the wrapping, and it was two sets of rings.

"Baby, see if you can fit this." Kay said rushing over to him.

Jermaine looked startled, like oh wow, what is this? But he also noticed she had a set as well.

"I know it's soon, but when you're ready to propose to me, they'll be ready. You can give these rings to your grandmother to hold onto, so when you're ready, we'll have them." Kay smiled at him.

Jermaine was in shock and alarmed as well, but didn't want to give off the wrong message.

"Okay." He replied. "So you want to be Mrs. Taylor?"

"One day soon, yes." Kay answered him with a smile."

The situation was crazy. Even the children were shocked. Jermaine and Kay had only been together for four weeks and two days. Well it was obvious she didn't feel love had a time limit on it.

In the meanwhile, the text messages, and unknown calls kept popping off, but Jermaine kept ignoring them. He started going through his phones, staring at old photos of him and Tamar that should have been deleted. And of Kadisha, and breast shots of Ms. Johnson. But now he had all these random couple shots of him and Kay.

'Wow.' He thought to himself. 'Maybe this is it. Maybe this crazy too good to be true thing, just might pop off.'

But something deep down inside told him to observe her just a little bit more. That's when he decided to call back the last unfamiliar number on his phone.

"Hello? Who is this?" Jermaine questioned when the caller picked up.

"I said I wasn't going to call you, and let you live your life. But people coming at me saying they're seeing you all over town with the cake lady."

"Shhhh.... Kadisha."

"Why you say my name all like that?" Kadisha replied tartly. "You act like you can't stand me now, when I did nothing but show you love." She said to him, genuinely hurt.

"Look, I don't want to argue with you." Jermaine replied in frustration. "And I don't care who you have spying on me around town. Me and you are not and were not together."

"Well from what I hear, she's not what you think." Said Kadisha.

"Well I'm around her every day, so you can't tell me no B.S. Kadisha." Jermaine said angrily.

"Well I went on a date and I liked it." Kadisha said, unperturbed by his attitude. "But we didn't have sex. He was really nice to me, and works for the government and has a lot going on."

"So what? Your point?" Jermaine shrugged.

"I'm just saying, I can get over you and we can still be friends."

"Well it looks like to me you're trying to make me jealous. But really that shhh doesn't move me." Jermaine said offhandedly. "Well I'm happy for you, and I hope it works out for you Kadisha."

"Why are you being such an ass?" Kadisha lashed out at him. "Being mean to me? Karma is going to most definitely hit you in the end."

"Why would Karma hit me when I done nothing wrong to you? We both agreed on moving on, which I did, and you can't take it and wishing things on me."

That's when Kadisha came on a bit aggressively.

"Hold up. I'm not one of these hood rat b$**h that you can just come off at! Besides, I got my own. I work for everything I've got. However, you're the only one I've ever considered being with, on the level you're on. I'm used to talking to businessmen, not no thugs."

"Well I tell you what? You go and be with the niggaz and quit calling and texting my phone." Then Jermaine hung it up in her ear. And watched his phone light up due to her constantly calling back and texting him.

Meanwhile, Jermaine got another random call from his daughter, De'dra. He picked it up.

"Hey dad, what'cha doing?" De'dra asked him.

"Nothing, what's been good with you baby?" He questioned her.

"Well dad, I heard that you're going to possibly marry the cake lady."

"Yeah, it's been discussed."

"Dad, you know it's only been a month, right? Since you both met."

"I know baby, I'm a just chill and see how this plays out, due to the fact that things are too perfect." Jermaine said with some caution.

"Dad just be careful." De'dra said quietly.

"I will, baby."

"Well okay dad, I just thought I'd call to check up on you. I got to work and do a double shift today, so love you, bye." De'dra hung up the phone, and Jermaine laid down on the couch in deep thought.

Like damn, Kadisha was really trippin. He gave her what she wanted, and that was being friends. Both of them agreed to just be friends and nothing further. Now she was hurt and feeling some type of way, trying to throw salt in his face. But Jermaine wasn't buying it. There was nothing in this world that was going to stand in his way, of who he chose to love. Because the cake lady was possibly it...wasn't she?

Chapter Nineteen

Watching her every move, the words she chose, Jermaine felt he had nothing to lose. Then he realized, hell naw, he's not going to risk the chance of having the perfect woman, or possible wife. The sex was good, the head was good, and the food she cooked was good.

She treated him like a King. He even started pulling out chairs and opening doors for this woman. She was just something different. And something else he would soon find out.

Going into the fifth week of their relationship, the cake lady, (AKA) Kay, had been doing many things Jermaine couldn't believe. She had already given him access to her bank account, keys to her car, bought him shoes, and also kept money in his pocket, and gas in his car. Ms. Cake lady was definitely trying to prove herself worthy of being a wife.

Whenever Jermaine would get frustrated, she would calm him down. Her word play was so crazy on how she would play it off. She knew exactly what would calm him down, no matter what time of day it would be.

Jermaine's soul would be swallowed. Not realizing that the devil also knew how to play off on him, and it was through women.

One day, Kay came to him frustrated, on what was supposedly said to her about her ex-boyfriend. So she told him she decided to go to him to put some closure to all of it.

But when she returned, she came back on something else, and Jermaine could see it in her face, that it wasn't good.

Part Seven

Hard to Breathe

Chapter Twenty

"we need to talk, and I don't want you to think any other way towards me at all, but I just have the tendency of screwing up people's lives." Kay said to him when she returned back from seeing her ex. She busted out in tears.

Jermaine was confused.

"What are you talking about?" He asked her.

"I talked to my ex-boyfriend, the one that was talking about killing himself, and I don't want you getting hurt." Kay said to him.

"Really." Jermaine said, watching her.

"Yes. He watches your live videos on Facebook, and knows when you're at my house, and when you're gone. I just need some time, due to everything is so complicated right now."

Right then and there, Jermaine knew what time it was. Due to he had heard the words, 'it's complicated' several times with both his ex-wives, and things went down hill.

He looked her directly in the eyes.

"So Kay, things are complicated now?" He said with a clipped voice. "Love isn't complicated, unless you still have love for him, while in love with me. Or is it the other way around?"

"You see this is exactly what I'm talking about." Kay said in tears. "I just need some time, cause you judging me already. I'm in love with you, and yes, I do still have love for him."

"Well I tell you what. If he got your heart, and I just have your mind, go back to him. Because if I can't have all of you, I don't want none of you." Jermaine laid his cards out.

Kay began to cry tremendously, and said to him, "Just give me some time to think." Then she jumped in her car and sped off in tears.

The following day, Kay came over to Jermaine's house and sat in front of him in silence, all teary eyed. Things most definitely were changing. Just as fast as things were taking place, when love was growing in the beginning. It was moving just as fast at being torn apart.

Kay stayed over all day and night, til that morning. Didn't nothing take place that night due to the tension of her being so stressed. And then being drunk as well.

Jermaine just held her one last time, due to he could almost tell that this would be their last night together. So that morning, Jermaine simply eased his way over to her side of the bed, and banged her out like it was the end of the world. Then she took back her car keys, and gave him back his key, and walked out of the house.

Later that day, Jermaine's phone rang. He looked down at the number, but didn't recognize it. But he answered it anyway.

"Hello?"

"Hey, I'm sorry to bother you, but could you ask your son Sencier could he cut the boys hair for me?"

It was Kadisha.

"Yes, I'll let him know. I'm pretty sure he'll do it." Jermaine replied.

"My kids ask about you all the time, Jermaine. You could at least say hello or something, instead of disappearing on them like you did." Kadisha said quietly.

"Well I'm about to be out, Kadisha okay?" Jermaine said sarcastically.

"Damn, it's like that? Really?" She said, hurt.

"No, it's not girl. I'll stop by there on my way to my father's house, just for a quick second. To say hello"

"Okay." Kadisha replied, sounding pleased.

Jermaine jumped into his car and headed to the store first, to grab him a square to have on the way. Finally he made it to her driveway, and put out the square, and took a deep breath.

It's been close to two months since he'd seen Kadisha, and the crazy words that were tossed back and forth sort of made him feel ashamed. But here goes nothing.

Jermaine knocked on the door twice, and before he could even knock a third time, the door was opened.

"Hey...." Kadisha said, as she appeared in the doorway.

"Hey." Jermaine replied, looking at her.

Kadisha yelled up the stairs for the kids to come down and see him.

"Hey guys, come downstairs and see your surprise!" She shouted in excitement.

The very second the kids saw him, they rushed him. They had missed him so much. It was crazy, unheard of. The kids began questioning Jermaine, about where he's been, and why he hasn't been around. And one of the kids actually said, "did my mother run you off?"

It was a little bit late, and due to it being a school night, Kadisha sent the kids upstairs to bed soon.

"Well I guess this is it." Jermaine said, preparing to go.

"So you're just gonna leave? You can't sit for a moment?" Kadisha asked him with a smile.

He sat back down.

"You're looking good, I see. Keeping yourself all up." Jermaine complimented her.

"Yes. I've got to, cause ever since you left, I've been feeling down." Kadisha responded.

"Why you been feeling down?" Jermaine wanted to know.

"You just don't know. The pillows, the blankets that you were laying on, I could still smell your cologne on them. There's been days I couldn't eat or sleep in my own bed, cause I've been missing you."

Jermaine paused, looking at her.

"What are you saying?" He asked her.

Kadisha took a deep breath.

"I'm not the one that hurt you. I would never hurt you. I'm not Juanita, and I'm not Tamar, or anyone else that hurt you."

She said this, as the tears rolled down her cheeks. Jermaine stared deeply into her eyes, and leaned towards her.

"I never said you have, or were any of those broads." He said gently.

"Then why did you up and leave so fast? And jump into a relationship with the cake lady?" Kadisha smiled as if she was trying to add a little humor.

141

"I felt that there could never be anything between us. You were friends with Tamar, even though she found out about us. But I always knew you felt some type of way, so I pushed on."

"Friends don't hook friends up with people they once slept with, and I don't know what Tamar considers a friend, but I would never do that to her." Kadisha stated.

"Well why all of a sudden you're telling me all this?" Jermaine asked her, confused.

"Because what I'm trying to tell you, Jermaine, is that I love you." She said the words breathlessly. "I love you, and I knew that I loved you the very second you walked away from me, and I truly love you now."

Jermaine knew for a fact that she was for real, because she'd said it with passion, and with heart. He felt it through his soul. He was moved.

"Wow...well I have a confession to make as well." Jermaine said to her.

"What?" Kadisha wanted to know.

"I love you too. But I didn't think you even felt that way about me. I didn't until I realized how much I couldn't get you off my mind."

"What about the cake lady?" Kadisha asked him.

"What about her?" Jermaine shrugged. "She told me her love is complicated, and I can feel where she really wants to be."

"Look, I don't want to be nobody's jump off." Kadisha said with hesitation.

"We could start over again as friends. Nothing more. I'm not looking at you as a jump off. Not ever." Jermaine meant those words.

"Well I gotta get up and get out of here, to go see my father." He prepared to go.

"I almost forgot about you going to see him." Kadisha responded, getting up with him.

"Are you going to come back afterwards?" She asked him with a smile.

"Why you say that?" Jermaine gave her a smirk.

"Cause I really don't want you to leave." Kadisha said softly. She was staring at him with those big sexy bedroom eyes.

She didn't have to say anything else.

Jermaine dropped his coat, walked over to her, and began kissing the soul out of both of them.

Stay tuned for

The Bouquet

II

By Ricky Boone

About The Author

Born in Saginaw Michigan but raised in Grand Rapids Michigan, Ricky Boone discovered his passion for writing when he was 14 years old. He attempted to write his first book based on his love for movies.

"I've always seen part two and three even before they were created. However, I watched a movie called 'Under the Cherry Moon' by Prince, and the poetry he wrote in the movie inspired me, and I've been hooked ever since."

Author Ricky Boone links into many poets such as Desiree Renea, a poet that was dedicated into ministry in the church. She introduced him, and he stood up in front of the congregation. Later on, he started following Black Ice, which was another poet as well that gave Ricky Boone the push he needed.

Afterwards he joined a group on Facebook called The Inner Circle, which was ran by Kesha Murphy and king Judah. Both were erotic and love poets who asked Ricky to collaborate with them, which sparked a flame that drew him into a totally new audience. This eventually caused Ricky Boone to start writing out his emotions and experiences. "Through my marriages, whether it was on a positive or negative level, I figured why give up on love; because it hasn't given up on me. I started to desire certain things, wanting to share with that special person, and thought well...I know I can't be the only one who desires these things. By the end of my divorce in 2017, which I thought would have broken me, I learned to channel that pain into what I wanted in a woman, and how I wanted her to treat me. And that was the birth of my first book, pillow talk."

Now, Author Ricky Boone has taken his success to the next level, in urban erotica and drama, with his books: Juice Box, and The Bouquet.

To learn more about Author Ricky Boone and his creatively written works and upcoming books, visit the publishing website.

www.AJBPublishiing.com